Instructions for using this book:

1. Enjoy reading the book!

2. Download the 'RainbowMe Kids' app, for Android or iPhone.

3. Select the 'O is for Oshun' book and point the tablet or phone at the character on each page.

4. Watch the characters come to life!

THIS BOOK IS DEDICATED TO MY PARENTS, AND MY FAMILY. THANK YOU FOR YOUR LOVE AND THANK YOU FOR SUPPORTING MY DREAMS, NO MATTER HOW FAR-FETCHED THEY MAY HAVE SEEMED.

KYA J.

First paperback edition December 2019

Book design by Danh Tran
Augmented Reality animation by The Intellify

ISBN 978-0-578-61163-1 (hardcover)

www.rainbowmekids.com

O is for Oshun

An ABC book of folklore characters from around the world

Written By: Kya Johnson

Illustrated by: Danh Tran

AR Animation: The Intellify

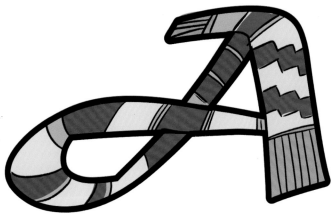

is for Afiong the proud princess, whose need for perfection landed her in a mess.

 is for Basilio,
the beetle rewarded for winning
the race.

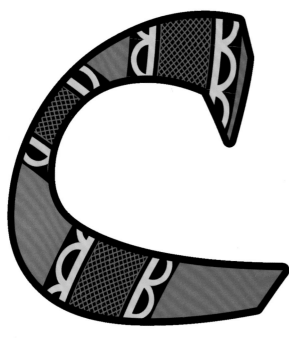

is for the Calabash kids, fruit that came to life to take care of Shindo's place.

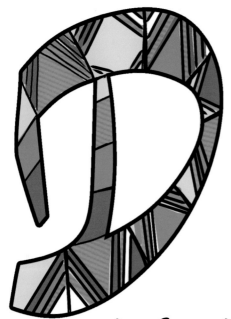

is for Demane and Demanzana,
the twins who got in trouble over meat.

 is for Efriam Duke, the king with a magic drum beat.

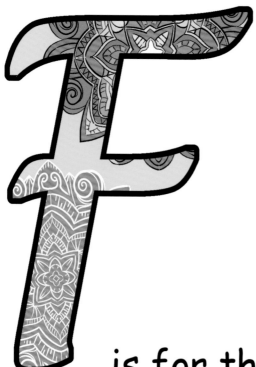 is for the Fakir who granted the lonely King's wish, for a price.

is for Guimara the giant
who became small for life.

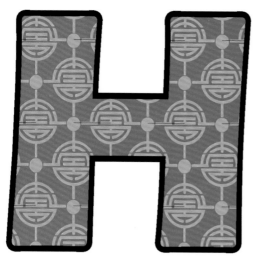 is for Hou Yi, the archer whose wife flew to the moon.

I is for Ishtar, the goddess who felt a lot of gloom.

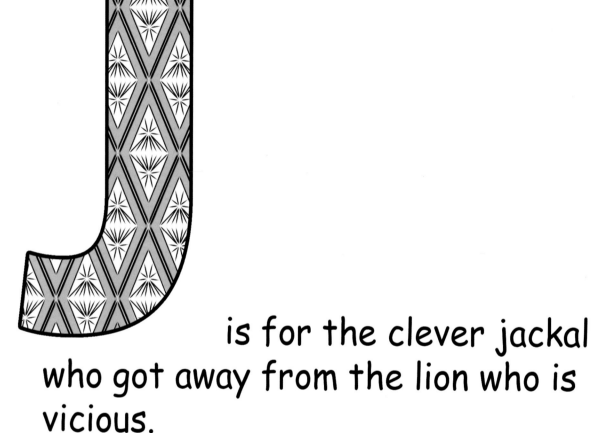

is for the clever jackal who got away from the lion who is vicious.

 is for Kofi Amero
the mean man who squandered
his wishes.

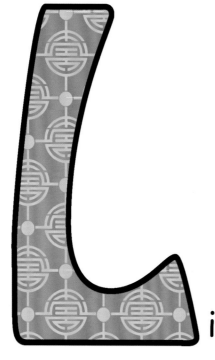 is for Lai the poor farmer who fell in love with a fairy.

 is for Momotaro

the conquerer of demons, how scary!

 for the Nsasak Bird

who is an animal kingdom leader

is for Oshun the goddess
of water and love to all who heed her.

is for the Parsley Queen
handpicked to be so by Prince Shotoku.

Q is for Quetzalcoatl, the god who became a man and was tricked into drinking pulque.

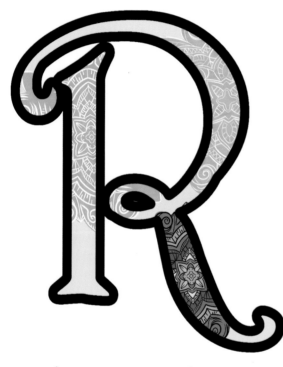 is for Raja Rasalu,

the prince who at age 12 was a precocious fella.

 is for the silver bell,

whose magic protected Princess Mirabella.

 is for Itiba Tahuvava, the woman whose sons created the sea.

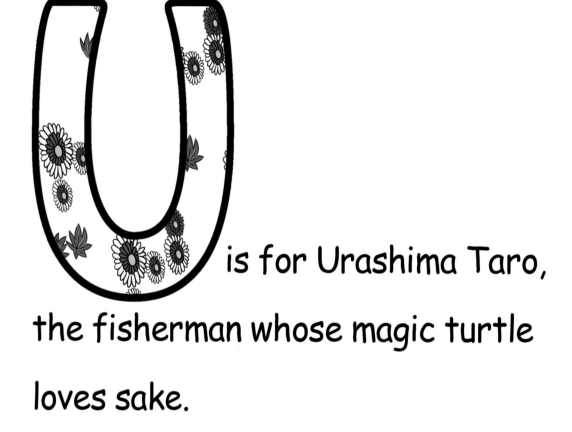 is for Urashima Taro, the fisherman whose magic turtle loves sake.

 is for the Vanara the creatures who can change their shape. They can be any animal, like a bear, or an ape.

 is for Wati-Kutjara, the lizard brothers who gave every animal its name.

 is for Xbalanque

one of the hero twins who avenged

their father's name.

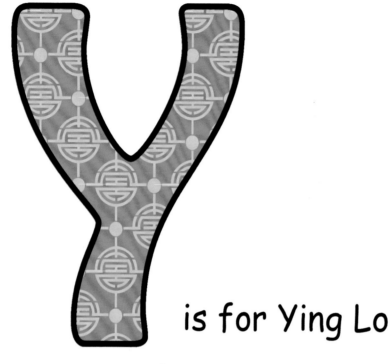

is for Ying Lo, the phantom vessel sent on a voyage above.

 is for Zhu Ying Tai,
the girl who turned into a butterfly
for love.

You have learned our names from A to Z, now listen below to hear all of our stories!